Five Mile, an imprint of
Bonnier Publishing Australia
Level 6, 534 Church Street, Richmond, Victoria 3121
www.fivemile.com.au

CIP data is available from the
National Library of Australia

First published 2015

Printed in China 5 4 3 2 1

FOXTROT

BY BECKA MOOR

The Five Mile Press

FOXTROT loved to dance.

He DANCED out of bed and into the bathroom.

He BOOGIED while he combed his whiskers

and TWIRLED as he brushed his teeth.

He DANCED as he dressed and did SPLITS as he put on socks.

He JUMPED and JIVED and swung and swayed until his disco clock told him it was time for breakfast.

He **TANGOED** with his toast and **MAMBOED** with his marmalade.
There was nothing Foxtrot could not foxtrot to.
Life was music to his ears.

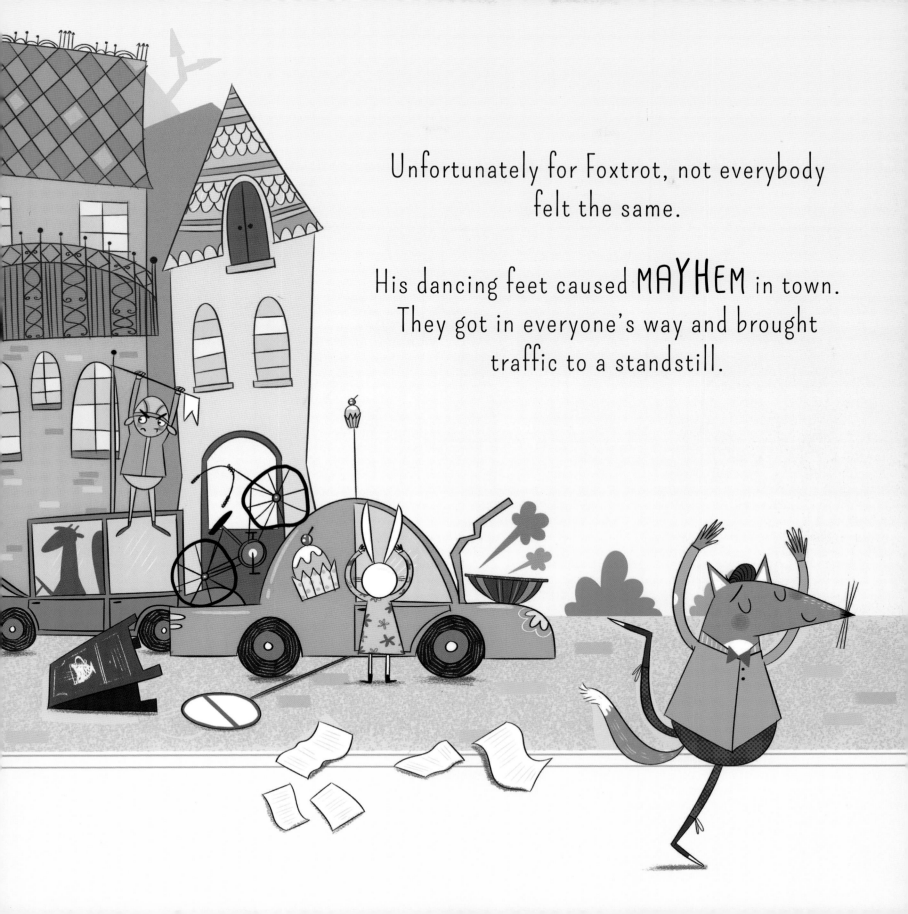

Unfortunately for Foxtrot, not everybody
felt the same.

His dancing feet caused MAYHEM in town.
They got in everyone's way and brought
traffic to a standstill.

They caused **CALAMITIES** in stores, knocking things over and annoying all the customers.

They caused pandemonium at parties
and CHAOS everywhere he went.

Eventually, Foxtrot's friends decided they
just HAD to tell him how much trouble his
dancing feet were causing.

Poor Foxtrot didn't understand. He
thought everyone loved his DANCING!

But how wrong he was.
His BOOGYING had to stop. But how?

His friend Rory tried tying Foxtrot's shoelaces together.

But Foxtrot couldn't stay still for very long
and kept FALLING over.

Bernard the Bear stuck
Foxtrot's feet to the floor
with Mr B's super
strong and
STICKY
honey.

But Foxtrot got **LONELY** standing all by himself.

HONEY

Eventually, Foxtrot decided that enough was enough.
There must be something else he would enjoy
as much as he enjoyed dancing.

So he tried rock climbing.
But Foxtrot soon discovered that he was
PETRIFIED of heights.

He tried acting, but he kept forgetting his lines.

Poor Foxtrot got **BOOED** off the stage.

He even tried drag-racing,
but it was far too fast
and made him feel all WOOZY.

All Foxtrot wanted to do was DANCE.

One morning, Foxtrot dragged himself out of bed and shuffled into the bathroom.

He **SIGHED** while combing his whiskers and **HUFFED** as he put on socks. He heaved and stumbled and moaned as he slowly got ready for breakfast.

As Foxtrot nibbled on his dry toast, he noticed something out of the corner of his eye.

It was a picture of him and his dance teacher. Mrs Flamenco had grown too old to run her school, but Foxtrot missed it very much.

Just as he was about to head back to bed, Foxtrot had a **BRILLIANT** idea.

"I will run the school!" he said, much to his friends' bewilderment.
"Then I can DANCE as much as I like, whenever I like!"

His friends weren't so sure that
Foxtrot's plan would work.

Still, they decided to lend a helping hand.

After a fresh coat of paint, Foxtrot's school was ready to open.
He couldn't wait to show it off.

Foxtrot held a HUGE opening ceremony and invited
everyone he knew to come and see his new dance school.

Foxtrot's friends were impressed. And when they saw how happy dancing made Foxtrot, they all signed up for his classes. Soon, everyone learned to **LOVE** dancing.

But no one could DANCE quite like Foxtrot.
And I don't think anyone ever will.